Take a Ball and Jump

and Other Stories

Written by Rob Childs

Illustrated by Liz McIntosh

Contents

Take a Run and Jump
1

'Before we start, girls, I want you to welcome a newcomer to our gym club.'

The teacher knew she didn't really have to draw their attention to the person standing next to her. All eyes had been glued on James the moment he'd stepped into the hall.

'B...but he's a boy!' came a shocked voice.

'Ten out of ten for observation, Katie,' Mrs Smith remarked as the other girls giggled. 'James has done a lot of gymnastics at his old school. I'm hoping we might soon have more boys wanting to join in here.'

Katie didn't like the sound of that at all. She rated herself the best gymnast in the club and hated the idea of some boy coming in and taking that title from her.

Right through the warm-up, the girls kept sneaking glances across to James, eager to see how good he was. He made the bending and stretching exercises look easy.

'Come on, Katie, concentrate,' Mrs Smith called out. 'Let's see a bit more effort from you. Don't be sloppy.'

Katie jumped. She wasn't used to being told off in gym. When the teacher ordered them into pairs to practise their balances, Katie headed straight for her usual partner.

'No, Katie, you work with James today, please. We don't want him to feel left out, do we?'

Katie's heart sank. She knew everybody was sniggering at her as she slowly made her way towards him. James gave her a shy, lopsided grin, but she stuck out her tongue and sat on the mat, sulking.

It was just then that two leering faces appeared outside one of the hall windows. It was Carl and his gang.

'There he is!' scoffed Carl. 'Told you so, Russ. Told you I'd heard that new kid ask Smithy about joining her stupid gym club.'

Russell sniggered. 'Yeah, just look at him sitting with that bossy Katie and all them girls. What a cissy!'

'Who wants to go rolling about all over the floor and standing on your head and stuff like that?' Carl sneered. 'There must be something wrong with him.'

They caught James's attention and pulled faces at him before Mrs Smith shooed them away.

'What's up with them?' he asked.

Katie smirked. 'They reckon gym is just for girls. Bet they'll be out to get you now they've seen you in here.'

James shrugged. 'They'll have to catch me first.'

2

'You first or me?' James asked. 'If we sit here chatting much longer, Mrs Smith might think that you fancy me!'

Katie blushed as red as her leotard and immediately stood up to do a handstand. 'And I don't need any support from you either,' she warned him.

James watched as Katie made a complete hash of her first attempt, overbalancing clumsily.

'Hey! Pretty good,' he chuckled.
'I'm impressed.'

'You're putting me off,' she
scowled. 'OK then, superstar, let's see
how brilliant you are.'

'I'm not too hot at balances either,' he admitted. 'I prefer vaulting. That's more exciting.'

Even so, he kicked up quite smoothly into a handstand. It was a little wobbly, but he held the position long enough before letting himself back down under control.

Katie bit her lip. She sensed already that she had more than met her match. And she knew it for sure when the time came for vaulting.

She was amazed at the speed of James's run-up to the springboard and the extra height he gained in his jumps.

So was Mrs Smith. The teacher was standing at the side of the vaulting box, ready to support the gymnasts as they went over. James took her by surprise with the power of his first jump. She could not get out of the way in time and he almost knocked her over.

Katie wasn't the only one to be watching enviously. Carl had rounded up a few more members of his gang and their noses were all squashed up against the windows.

'Wow! He can sure jump!' gasped Mark.

Carl pulled him away. 'Never mind that. We're here to teach this big cissy a lesson,' he snarled, punching his fist fiercely into his other hand for effect. 'I reckon we can change his mind about doing gym, don't you, gang?'

As James set off for home across the playground later, a shout came from behind some bushes near the fence.

'Hey, you! Wanna borrow my sister's leotard?'

James didn't answer. He was too busy trying to make out how many figures there were in hiding.

Carl stepped out into view. 'What do you think you're doing, prancing around in that gym club?'

'Why? What's it got to do with you?'

'I'm asking the questions. You can just go and take a run and jump.'

'Sounds like a good idea,' James said as four others appeared, blocking his path to the gate.

Before any of them could move to stop him, he ran full tilt at the fence and did an enormous leapfrog right over the top of it.

Landing safely on the other side, he hurried away down the footpath towards the main road without even bothering to glance back.

What would you have done if Carl's gang tried to stop you on your way home?

3

For weeks after his spectacular escape, James had to suffer the boys' taunts. Then, to their surprise, they discovered that he was a good footballer as well as a gymnast.

They even began to let him join in their lunchtime football games.

'You'll have to play for the school team next season,' said Mark. 'We need someone quick like you on the wing.'

'And the way you throw yourself about, bet you'd make a great goalkeeper too,' added Russell.

Carl was not pleased. He prided himself on being the school's best all-rounder at sports and he regarded James as an unexpected rival. He brooded over the problem, but it was Katie who came up with the possible solution.

She sidled up to Carl one day in the playground. 'Are you just as fed up with James as I am?' she said. 'He's always showing me up in gym.'

'Yeah, he's getting right up my nose too. I don't want him winning everything on Sports Day.'

'Listen,' said Katie slyly. 'I've got an idea how we can teach him a lesson.'

'Go on, I'm listening,' he said, suspicious of what Katie might be up to. Normally, they never even spoke to each other, apart from to argue.

'You know how good you are at long jump...'

Carl nodded eagerly. The long jump was his favourite event. It was no secret that he intended to smash the school record on Sports Day. He'd been boasting about it for months.

'If we made sure James did the long jump on Sports Day, you could really put him in his place,' said Katie. 'I mean, you're unbeatable at that. He wouldn't stand a chance.'

Katie's face was a picture of mischief.

She could tell that Carl was tempted, and it didn't take much more flattery to persuade him to agree to her plan. Then she went off to find James.

'What!' he exclaimed when Katie suggested he went in for the long jump event. 'I've never even tried it before.'

'Nothing to it. Just like running up to do a vault.'

James wasn't convinced. 'Why are you so keen on me doing the long jump all of a sudden?'

'To pay Carl back for going on at us about gymnastics like he does,' she replied. 'This'd be a great chance to show him up in front of all his mates.'

'Why should I want to do that?' he said. 'Anyway, I'd have to beat him first. Sounds like he's brilliant.'

'He's all mouth! Bet you could outjump him easily.'

James shrugged. He wasn't at all sure just which one of them Katie really wanted to see end up with a red face.

How did Katie plan to put James in his place?

4

'Where's the springboard?' James asked jokingly as he arrived at the long jump pit.

'This ain't the gym,' Carl sneered. 'No nice bouncy springboard out here. We just run up and jump. Watch me. You're in for a surprise.'

It was PE and everyone was practising for Sports Day. James still hadn't decided whether to do the long jump; he wanted to try it out first.

Carl charged up to take a jump. He built up some speed and launched himself through the air.

'Wow!' said Russell. 'Great jump!'

'Just a warm-up,' Carl grinned, and then pointed to the deep hollows that his feet had left in the sand. 'Right, now it's your turn. Let's see you beat that.'

James did his best. He sprinted forward, gathering speed quickly, but his take-off was a disaster.

He landed in an untidy heap in the sand. He could hear the laughter and jeers as he shakily got to his feet like a new-born giraffe.

'Hmm … not as easy as it looks,' he grunted, spitting some sand out of his mouth. 'I'm going to need a bit of time to get the hang of this event.'

'C'mon, Carl. Show us how you're gonna break the record on Sports Day,' urged Mark.

Carl shook his head. He didn't want to risk putting James off too much.

Katie kept a close eye on James as he trained. He worked hard to improve his take-off technique.

'Getting better,' she said. 'You are going to enter the long jump event, aren't you?'

James laughed. 'You seem pretty keen for me to enter. I wonder why?'

'Well, are you going to or not?' demanded Carl. 'C'mon, I dare you. Or are you too chicken to take me on?'

It was a challenge that James couldn't resist.

'OK, I must be mad, but anything to shut you two up,' he grinned. 'Besides, it's good fun, this long jumping. I've always enjoyed flying through the air.'

He just wasn't very keen on falling flat on his face.

'May the best man win!' Katie cried, sniggering to herself as she jogged away. 'And I can't lose out, whatever happens. One of them is bound to be made to look a fool.'

Sports Day began well for Katie as she won her first race, in style. Then she hurried over to where Carl and James were competing. There was quite a crowd around the long jump pit. Carl and James had already had the first of their three attempts.

'How are they doing?' Katie gasped out to Russell.

'Carl's way in the lead, but he's not got the record yet,' he replied.

'I'm not bothered about that,' she snapped. 'What about James?'

'He no-jumped,' Russell smirked. 'His foot was well over the take-off line.'

Katie watched James place a stick to mark where he should start off from for his run-up. She also saw that when James's back was turned, Carl had wandered up and casually kicked the stick away.

5

Carl's second attempt was also judged to be a no-jump.

'Sorry, your toes were just over the line, I'm afraid,' Mrs Smith told him kindly, knowing how much the record meant to Carl.

What she didn't know about were all the hours of secret training in the evenings. Carl knew he could beat the record. He'd already done so twice in practice.

Carl slumped down on the grass, disappointed, while other boys had a turn – until James appeared. He stood up to get a clear view and chuckled at the sight of his rival looking round in vain for the marker stick.

James took a shorter run than most but it was very fast. Although he took off a bit early, he still soared into the air.

Carl waited anxiously as Mrs Smith measured the jump. When the distance was announced, it was only five centimetres behind his own. The record was in danger, not just from him, but from James as well.

Carl knew that he now had a real fight on his hands. He glanced towards Katie and caught her eye. She was smirking at him.

'Huh! This is all your fault,' he muttered.

The final round of jumps began and the crowd hushed as Carl stood ready to run up for his jump.

'It's now or never,' he murmured under his breath. 'I'm going to break that record!'

Carl thundered up to the line. He took off at exactly the right place and gained tremendous lift.

After landing in the sand, he bounced back up on to his feet immediately. He sensed he'd got everything just right. He danced around the pit, whooping with excitement, not caring what anybody thought.

'A new school record!' announced Mrs Smith proudly. 'Four metres and eight centimetres. Well done, Carl. Very few people your age can break the four metre barrier.'

James went over to shake his hand. 'Fantastic jump!' he said, smiling. 'You're the champ.'

Carl grinned in triumph, but he was soon in for a shock.

As James prepared for his last jump, he had nothing to lose. 'I'll just give it everything I've got,' he decided.

He did exactly that. It was a huge jump. James seemed to hang in the air for an age before he stretched out his legs as far forward as possible on landing.

Carl gasped in relief when he saw James put a hand down into the sand behind him to stop himself falling backwards. Mrs Smith had to measure to where his fingers touched, not where his footprints were.

'What a pity, James,' Mrs Smith said. 'It was below four metres, but you still beat the old record!'

Carl went over to congratulate him. 'Perhaps there is something in this gym lark after all, if it helps you to leap like that. Might even be willing to give it a try myself now!'

Some of the other lads were quick to agree.

'Reckon a spot of gym training might help to make me fitter for football,' said Russell.

'Any chance of me joining the club as well?' asked Mark.

James was astonished. 'Well, we could sure do with more boys in the gym club.'

Katie's face fell a mile. All her scheming had totally backfired.

'Serves me right,' she sighed to herself. 'Looks like I'll have to keep on my toes now with all that lot around, never mind James!'

Carl turned to James. 'Hardly dare think how close you came to beating me,' he said.

James laughed. 'Guess I was simply following that piece of advice you gave me a while ago.'

'What do you mean?' said Carl, puzzled.

'All I did was just take a run and jump!'

What did James mean when he said, 'All I did was just take a run and jump'?

Do you think Carl and James will be friends from now on?

Catches Win Matches
1

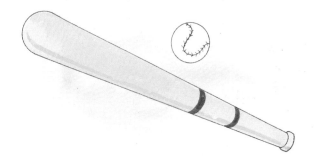

'Butterfingers!'

'What a dolly! He couldn't even catch a bus!'

'Bet he couldn't even catch a cold!'

Jason shrugged off the insults. What did he care if he wasn't any good at sport? He'd much rather be at home on the farm, helping to look after the animals. Yet here he was instead, after school, taking part in an extra rounders practice on the playing field.

Jason could hardly believe it, and neither could the rest of the class. Every time he did something wrong – which was whenever the ball came anywhere near him – they complained loudly to the teacher.

'He can't hit the ball, Miss.'

'He can't throw the ball, Miss.'

'He can't catch the ball, Miss.'

'Does Jason *have* to play, Miss?' cried Rachel, loudest of all.

'Rachel!' Miss O'Brien answered

her sharply. 'You know full well why he does.'

Jason sighed. It was all Michael's fault really. But Michael was his friend so what could he do?

He watched as Michael peered through his thick glasses, face screwed up tight with the effort. Michael's eyesight was so poor, he wasn't even sure whether the batter was a boy or a girl.

In class, Michael used a special magnifying glass to see his work better. Jason sat next to him and often acted as an extra pair of eyes to let Michael know what was going on elsewhere in the room.

But this time, Jason reckoned, Michael had finally gone too far.

Michael wanted to be in the rounders team to play a challenge match against another class: and he could be very stubborn, once he'd made his mind up about something. Not even Miss O'Brien could put him off the idea when he first heard about it.

'Do you really think you'd be able to cope, Michael?' she began gently, trying not to hurt his feelings. 'I mean…'

Her voice had trailed away as she saw the eager smile on his face.

'Jason will help me, Miss. He's good at helping me. He's like my own personal guide dog!'

'Woof!' barked Jason and they all laughed.

Under his breath, however, Jason groaned. He was already fearing the worst. 'Oh thanks a lot, pal. Now you've really gone and done it!'

2

When Rachel, and her friend
Kiran, learned that Michael wanted
to try for the rounders team, they
were fed up. They cornered Daniel
in the playground.

'We've got no chance in this match
if those two clowns play,' Rachel
moaned.

'You're the best rounders player,
what are you going to do about it?'
Kiran demanded.

Daniel pulled a face. 'Not up to me.
Miss O'Brien is picking the team.'

'Can't you say something?' pleaded Rachel. 'Michael will need a football to hit, not a little rounders ball.'

'He doesn't even know where the ball is half the time,' sneered Kiran.

'Don't worry,' Daniel chuckled. 'I bet Jason will find a way to wriggle out of it before it's too late.'

Jason did try; but in the end even Michael was getting fed up with his long list of excuses.

'Look, I know you think sports are a waste of time, but this may be the only chance I'll ever get to play in a proper match.'

Jason gave in, feeling guilty. 'OK, don't go on about it. If it's that important to you, let's give it a try.'

Michael let out a whoop of joy. 'That's great, Jason, you're a real mate. I knew you wouldn't let me down.'

Jason managed to raise a weak smile. That's just what he was worried about.

He didn't want his own clumsiness spoiling things for Michael.

'C'mon, then, we'd better get some practice in,' he said. 'I reckon I need it more than you!'

Michael borrowed a rounders bat and ball from his older sister and they took it in turns to bowl to each other in his back garden. It was not a success.

The ball was just a blur to Michael

and Jason was not exactly the best batter in the world.

He wasn't even the best batter in the garden when Sharon came out to join them. She kept belting the ball over the fence into a field of playful cows. Jason didn't mind that; each time he went to fetch it, he took longer to return. Sharon got bored and disappeared inside again.

The boys carried on for a while.

Jason shouted, 'Now!' when he bowled to let Michael know the ball was coming, but it was no use. Michael swished the bat wildly through the air, either too early or too late to make contact.

'Just a matter of timing,' he said with determination. 'We'll soon get it sorted out.'

Jason wasn't so sure. It was perhaps just as well that Michael wasn't able to see the look of doubt on his friend's face.

How do you think Jason will help Michael to get better at rounders?

3

'I've been thinking,' said Jason the following day. 'Why don't we just work on your bowling and try to make that better?'

Sharon backed him up. 'It might be your best hope of being picked to play. Every rounders team needs a good steady bowler.'

'OK, let's give it a go,' Michael sighed. 'Doesn't seem like I'll ever get the hang of batting.'

Jason chalked a big white square on the garage wall as a target. Michael could barely see it, but Jason used the square to guide the bowler's aim.

'Throw the next one higher,' he'd direct him. 'And a bit more to the right.'

Sharon also showed Michael how to take a few steps before releasing the ball.

With practice, his jerky run-up became smoother and even Sharon began to find his bowling more difficult to hit. She rarely disturbed the cows in the field now – much to Jason's disappointment.

The next day, in PE, Jason was kept busy. Neither he nor Michael managed to hit the ball when they batted, but Jason had to pant alongside him each time Michael missed and set off on a run. Besides keeping his friend on course, he also had to call out whether to stop or move on to the next base. Michael couldn't tell where the ball had been thrown and it often became very confusing.

Once, Jason failed to look where he was going himself and knocked one of the fielders over. Unfortunately it happened to be Rachel.

'Can't you do *anything* right?' she snapped.

'I'm doing my best, aren't I?'

'Well, I just hope I'm not around when you're doing your worst!'

When their turn came to field, they would both chase after the ball together, but Jason left the throwing to Michael who had a stronger arm. It worked all right so long as Michael was pointed in the right direction.

'Please can I have a go at bowling, Miss?' Michael asked after a while.

Miss O'Brien was not too hopeful. 'Very well, Michael, you can't be any worse than the rest, I suppose,' she sighed. 'Everyone is bowling far too many no-balls.'

Michael began nervously, but Miss O'Brien liked the look of his flowing action. As his bowling became quicker and more accurate, she watched him with extra interest.

Only Daniel and Kiran managed to hit the ball well enough to score a rounder. With Jason close by to feed Michael the ball and pass on advice, their teamwork was impressive.

'Well done. I can see you've been having some secret practice!' Miss O'Brien praised them, making them blush. Then she broke the good news. 'I think you both deserve to be in the team – with Michael as our bowler!'

4

Michael hardly stopped grinning for the rest of the week – and neither did Imran, the captain of the other team.

Imran took great delight in taunting Daniel about the selection of Michael and Jason. 'We're going to thrash you now with that pair playing.'

'Don't count on it,' Daniel replied, fingers crossed behind his back. 'They're our secret weapons.'

Sadly, when the match began, Daniel's team got off to the worst possible start. Put into bat, Kiran was out first ball. She hit it straight to a fielder, who clung on well to the stinging catch.

Kiran lost interest in the game and spent most of the time practising her handstands against the fence until she saw Daniel open the scoring as he smacked the ball into the outfield.

'Rounder! Rounder! Rounder!' echoed the cheers as Daniel flew all the way round to reach home safely.

When Jason batted, he swung and missed – as usual – just scampering to first base before the ball beat him to it.

'Stay there!' squealed Rachel, trapped on second base and scared that Jason would keep going and run her out. He slammed on the brakes just in time, but stuck his tongue out to annoy her instead.

After helping Michael to complete the course in stages, Jason then found it was his turn to bat again. Still breathing heavily, he was as shocked as anyone when he made clean contact with the ball. In fact he was so stunned, that he simply stood in the batting square and gawked at the ball disappearing into the distance.

'Run, you idiot!' Kiran screamed. 'Go, go, go!'

He went. He hurtled round so fast that he almost overtook Rachel, the class sprint champion. As he touched fourth base, he collapsed to the ground in an untidy heap.

'Incredible!' laughed Daniel. 'You've actually scored a rounder. Well done!'

Jason's face lit up. It was his first-ever taste of sporting glory and it felt good.

But it couldn't last.

A short while after Rachel had scored a rounder too, Jason carelessly ran her out – and himself – by forcing her to run on to a post that had already been stumped.

Her temper flared, but he had no time to stand and argue. He still had to try and help Michael, who had somehow survived longer than most.

Michael missed the ball again and hared off towards first base with Jason hard on his heels. The throw was wild and Jason urged the runner on.

'Keep going, pal, they're messing it up,' he shouted.

Michael lost some ground by going too wide around second base. He was unable to turn left quickly enough in his excitement, but Jason realised he might yet make it home.

'Go on, all the way,' he cried.

As the final base came into Michael's blurred vision, the fielder panicked and fumbled the ball.

'Touch, touch!' Jason screamed, and Michael's outstretched bat hit the post an instant before the ball did. He was in!

Michael was mobbed in delight by the whole team and Daniel said, 'Great, that's a vital half rounder for us.'

Before their batting time was up, the captain added another full rounder to the score. It took the team's final total to six points.

Both teams enjoyed a much needed drink during the break between innings. Jason took a great gulp of water and then tipped some over his head to try and cool himself down.

'Well played, everybody,' smiled Miss O'Brien. 'Now we must bowl and field well too. Remember the old saying, *"Catches win matches"!*'

'Time for the demon bowler!' Jason grinned. 'Imran's lot gave away one and a half rounders with no-balls, so we'll have to watch out too.'

'I'll leave that to you,' Michael said, giving him a wink from behind his specs.

High and wide no-balls near the start of the innings did cost them half a rounder, but Michael soon found his range.

His confidence grew, and almost every delivery from then on went speedily towards its target.

Michael's skilful bowling tricked many of the batters into missing or getting themselves caught, but not Imran. Daniel knew that the captain was their biggest danger. Unless they got him out soon, Imran could win the match on his own with his powerful slogs. He had already scored two of his side's three rounders so far.

At last Imran mis-hit the ball. It soared into the air and Daniel rushed to get underneath it as it fell from the sky. He was the safest catcher in the team.

'Mine!' he shouted to keep other people out of his way.

Too late! Rachel was also heading for it, staking her own claim for the catch. Eyes fixed on the ball, they remained on collision course like guided missiles…

Crunch!!

The ball landed on the ground next to them, untouched, while Imran jogged past the bases for an easy rounder.

Daniel and Rachel were shaken up and winded, but lucky to escape serious injury. What hurt them most was the knowledge that the score was now up to $4\frac{1}{2}$ points.

Then Imran's team got another easy rounder. Kiran had been doing a handstand in the outfield between bowls and wasn't ready in time to stop the ball going past her. She hung her head in shame.

Jason warned Michael that Imran was coming in to bat again. 'They're only half a rounder behind now,' he said. 'Keep it low.'

Michael did as Jason said, but Imran still made good contact. He whacked it straight back – dead straight.

The bowler never saw it coming.

The hard rounders ball smacked right into his tummy, the force and surprise of it doubling him up. It knocked the air out of his body in a loud grunt and he keeled over backward, both hands clutching his middle.

Imran set off for what he thought would be the winning rounder. Everyone else rushed towards Michael in alarm as he lay flat out. They were amazed to find him smiling, his glasses tilted at an odd angle across his face.

'Are you all right?' Miss O'Brien asked, bending down to refix them.

Suddenly Michael held up the ball in triumph.

'He's out!' he cried. 'I caught him out!'

Miss O'Brien gasped. 'I wondered where the ball had gone to. It was in your hands all the time!'

Without Imran, there was no further scoring.

At the end, Daniel's team won by just half a rounder, 6 to $5\frac{1}{2}$.

'What a hero!' whooped Jason. 'That catch of yours was a match-winner.'

'Yeah,' Michael grinned. 'It was a real blinder!'

It took a moment for Jason to see the joke and then the two of them laughed until tears ran down their cheeks.

What do you think Michael will tell Sharon about how the match went?

Girl in Goal
1

'Can I play?'

The boys looked round in surprise. They were just about to pick sides for their lunchtime kickabout.

'Go on, let me play in goal.'

'You must be joking,' said Ben, captain of Gateway Juniors soccer team. 'Girls are no good at football. Clear off, Samantha.'

She stayed where she was.

'They called me Sam at my old school.'

The footballers grinned at each other and waited to see what Ben would do. He didn't want to be shown up by this new girl in front of all his mates. She was bigger than him and he didn't fancy the idea of trying to get rid of her by force.

He decided to give way – just a little.

'OK, then... I'll call you Sam,' he sighed, 'but you still can't play in our game.'

The boys all laughed and Sam went off to sulk against the nearby wall. But she was not the kind of girl to give up that easily. As soon as the game started, she wandered back to stand behind one of the goals.

Sam loved goalkeeping. Ever since she could remember, Dad had played football with her in the garden, taking shots at her in their home-made goal. Now she could catch a ball better than him!

Sam watched as different boys took their turn as goalie between the piles of coats. None of them, it seemed to her, really wanted to play in goal. Two even let in shots on purpose so they could go back out on the field.

Suddenly, Ben lashed in a beauty. It was struck with such power that the ball flew past the goalkeeper before he made a move.

But not past Sam! Out of habit, she leapt up and snatched the ball cleanly out of the air.

Her spectacular catch did not go unnoticed, although Ben was already well into his goal celebrations.

He danced away, punching the air, and then posed for the television cameras as if he'd just scored the winner at Wembley.

Gareth, the school team's centre-back, had seen Ben's antics before. He was staring in amazement towards Sam instead.

'Hey, maybe she's not too bad after all,' he thought, then checked himself. 'Well, for a girl, that is!'

2

When the bell went, the footballers trailed in for afternoon school and Sam plucked up the courage to confront Ben.

'What have you got against girls playing football?'

''Cos it's a man's game. It ain't meant for girls,' he snarled, brushing past her. 'Anyway, it's my ball. I can decide who I want to play with it.'

Sam realized that one of the boys was hanging back.

'Old Nozza runs the school footy team,' he said to her. 'You'll have to try and show him what you can do.'

'Nozza? Who's that?' she asked.

'His real name is Mr Norris. He used to teach here but now he's retired. He's dead keen on football so he still comes in to coach the team.'

'What's your name?' asked Sam.

'Gareth, but just call me Gaz. All my mates do.'

'Thanks, Gaz. What's the team like this season?'

Gareth chuckled. 'Gateway are the strongest team in the league. We're bottom, holding everybody else up!'

It was an old joke, but Sam still laughed.

'Sounds like you need some girls in it,' she grinned.

'Don't reckon old Nozza would approve,' he said, shaking his head. 'He's like Ben. They both think girls and football don't mix.'

'That's stupid. Loads of girls play for their schools at soccer nowadays.'

'The reason we're bottom of the league is 'cos we've been letting too many goals in. What the team really needs is a decent keeper...'

'Maybe there's hope for me,' said Sam, as they went into the classroom.

When Gareth sat down, Ben sneered at him. 'I saw you, talking to that girl. What have you been saying to her?'

'Nothing. Just telling her to bring her kit for PE tomorrow, that's all.'

'Netball kit, I hope.'

Much to Sam's disgust, she did have to play netball. She'd changed into her bright yellow goalie top, with matching cap and gloves, but her teacher insisted that she practised with the rest of the girls.

Sam watched with envy as Mr Norris led the boys over to the playing field. Ben pointed towards her and laughed.

She sighed and grabbed the red GK bib before anyone else could claim it. She was still determined to play as goalkeeper, even in netball.

Sam used her extra height to good advantage in the goal circle.

Nobody could outjump her and her catching was excellent. The shooter hardly had a touch of the ball.

The teacher was very impressed. 'To think you wanted to go off and play with the boys,' she laughed. 'What a waste! You're the best goal keeper of your age I've ever seen.'

It was a nice compliment, but Sam wished that Mr Norris had said it to her instead.

3

Ben was away the next day and Gareth invited Sam to play at lunchtime. The other boys didn't object. She was the only one who had brought a football to school.

Gareth picked Sam for his team immediately, causing an outbreak of giggles and jokes among his mates.

''She your girlfriend or something, Gaz?' smirked Jack, Gateway's leading scorer and rival team captain for the day.

'She's my goalkeeper,' he replied. 'Bet you don't score past her.'

'Easy. What d'yer want to bet?'

Gareth thought quickly. 'If you manage to score, you can have my new computer game for a week. And if you don't I can have one of yours.'

Jack grinned. 'OK, you're on. I'll come round to your place and collect it after school.'

'Right, Sam, you know what's at stake,' Gareth said.

'What, your game?'

'No, I don't care about that. This is your big chance to prove to this lot how good you are in goal.'

Jack tested her out straight away. His low shot bounced awkwardly in front of her, but Sam made sure her body was well behind the ball. It bobbled up, struck her on the shoulder and rolled wide of the coats.

'Good stop!' cried Gareth.

'Lucky, you mean,' snorted Jack. 'Next time, you wait.'

He soon found out that Sam's goalkeeping didn't rely on luck. She'd only been beaten once and Jack wasn't the scorer. Sam had pulled off several saves at his expense and her side were winning 4–1.

The longer the game went on, the redder Jack's face became with frustration and embarrassment.

Finally, his blushes were saved by the bell. Distracted for a moment by its loud rings, Sam let Jack's last desperate shot skid under her dive.

'Time was up. Doesn't count,' she yelled crossly.

'Rubbish!' Jack retorted. 'Game's not over till we pack up. That was a goal.'

'Doesn't matter, Sam, forget it,' Gareth told her. 'You've shown them what you can do, that's the main thing.'

'Yeah, but Nozza doesn't know yet,' she said.

Gareth grinned. 'Looks like we'll have to make sure he finds out. We've got a soccer practice tomorrow after school, so come prepared – and bring your cap.'

'My goalie cap? I don't see...'

'Nor will old Nozza,' Gareth laughed. 'I've just come up with a brilliant plan. Listen...'

4

'You say this newcomer is a useful goalkeeper,' said Mr Norris before the practice began.

'Yes,' said Gareth. 'Sam's the name. Played in goal at a previous school.'

Mr Norris gazed across to where Jack was taking shots at the tall figure in the yellow outfit. 'Hmm, seems to know how to handle a ball,' he murmured. 'Right, let's see what this er…Sam can do, shall we?'

Gareth breathed a sigh of relief and went to break the good news to her. 'OK so far. He doesn't suspect anything – yet. Just keep that cap pulled down real tight so old Nozza doesn't get a proper look at you.'

Jack laughed. 'Good job Ben's still away. We could never have tried to pull a stunt like this with him around.'

Mr Norris stood on the touchline to watch the practice match. Every so often, he'd blow his whistle to halt play and bellow at somebody for making a mistake.

Praise was rare, but he actually clapped when Sam dived full-length to tip a rising shot over the crossbar.

The boys could hardly believe it.

'He must like you,' chuckled Gareth.

'He won't when he finds out who Sam really is,' Jack cut in. 'He'll be dead mad, being made to look a fool.'

Sam had no chance to worry about that. She was kept much too busy, producing a number of fine saves. By the end of the session, her kit and face were smothered in mud.

'Not a pretty sight!' joked Gareth, just managing to dodge Sam's playful swipe in time.

Only once had her cap come off. It happened during a goalmouth scramble with Mr Norris standing nearby, but he had not seemed to notice anything strange.

'Home time, gather round,' he called out and the players trotted up to him, dying to hear what he was going to say about Sam. The trick seemed to have worked a treat.

'Er..have you picked the team for the next game yet, sir?' asked Gareth.

'You mean, will our new star goalie be playing?' said Mr Norris. Then he smiled and leant over to lift Sam's cap gently off her head.

'Of course. I've already heard all about Samantha's talents in netball. No reason why she can't play for Gateway in both sports, is there?'

Mr Norris strode off, whistling to himself, leaving a group of stunned footballers gaping at each other.

'It's us who've been made fools of,' laughed Gareth. 'Old Nozza must have known what we were up to all along.'

When Ben returned to school on Monday morning, he dashed straight for the sports noticeboard.

'Who's this S. *Roberts* in goal, Gaz?' he asked, staring at the teamsheet for the home game against Barton Primary. 'Is he some new kid?'

'Close,' said Gareth, barely able to keep a straight face. 'Look behind you.'

Ben turned to see Sam grinning at him from across the corridor.

'Don't be stupid,' he gasped out. 'Old Nozza would never pick a girl for the team...'

5

The Gateway players were already out on the pitch, warming up, when Barton arrived in a convoy of cars.

Sam was wearing her cap again. Her new team mates wanted to see the visitors' reactions, too, when they found out who was in goal.

Ben had been forced to accept the situation. He'd seen Sam in action now at lunchtime and was playing it cool, trying not to show that he'd been impressed by her ability.

This was a vital match for both schools. Gateway needed a win to lift them off the bottom of the league table while three points would put Barton on top.

The difference between the two teams was clear to see. Barton were full of confidence and expected to score every time they attacked. Gateway merely hoped to do so.

The main reason that the first half somehow remained goal-less was because of Sam. Barton just could not get the ball into her net. Every shot they had on target seemed to finish up in Sam's safe hands.

Sam was enjoying herself and felt on top form. One reflex save from a shot that deflected off Gareth's knee was quite superb.

'C'mon, guys, we can still win this,' Ben urged at half-time. But then Jack nudged him on the arm and Ben tried again. 'I mean guys and girl. Let's show this Barton lot we mean business.'

The captain tried to lead by example. He covered the whole pitch, supporting the attack and the defence. But with just ten minutes to go, Ben mistimed a tackle in the penalty box and caught an opponent on the heel. Down he crashed into the mud.

'Penalty!' cried the Barton players.

The referee pointed to the spot and Ben sat in a dejected heap until Gareth pulled him up on to his feet.

'It's not all over yet. They've still got to get it past Sam, remember.'

Ben found a sudden ray of hope. 'Sorry about the things I've said, Sam,' he apologized to her. 'You're a great goalie. It's up to you now to get us out of this mess.'

Sam managed a nervous smile. 'Wish me luck.'

'You don't need it. You're unbeatable today!'

All eyes were fixed on Sam. She settled herself on the line, tensed and ready to spring either way. As the kicker ran up she whipped off her hat and threw it out of the way.

'It's a girl!' someone shouted, just as the kicker made contact with the ball.

The loud cry might have put the boy off. His kick was sliced to Sam's right, but not out of her reach. She dived and got both hands to the ball, clutching it to her chest to make sure it didn't escape.

Ignoring the cheers, Sam belted
the ball upfield. She'd spotted Jack
in a space on the halfway line.

'Go, Jack, go,' she screamed. 'Go
for goal.'

Her swift action caught Barton by
surprise. Jack had been left unmarked
and he had no trouble dribbling past
the single defender who barred his way.

He now only had the goalkeeper
to beat and Jack relished this kind of
one-on-one duel. He sold the keeper
a dummy, leaving him helpless on
the ground, and then stroked the ball
into an empty net. 1-0 to Gateway.

Barton were not the same team after that. Sam had little more to do and Ben clinched their victory by scoring a second goal himself near the end.

At the final whistle, the captain was the first one to give Sam a big hug of delight. But he wasn't the last.

'You were brilliant!' Ben cried. 'Old Nozza's sure to make you "*Man of the Match*"!'

Sam gave him a funny look and he realized what he'd said. 'Well, you know what I mean,' he grinned sheepishly.

'Don't worry, we all know what you mean,' Gareth laughed. 'And it also means we won't finish bottom of the league – not now that we've got a girl in goal!'

Do you think girls and boys should be able to do any sport they want? Why?